The
Magic Top Mystery

by JANE and JIM O'CONNOR

illustrated by KEVIN CALLAHAN

SCHOLASTIC INC.
New York Toronto London Auckland Sydney Tokyo

Scholastic Books in the Pick-A-Path Series
How many have you read?

ISBN 0-590-33142-6

12 11 10 9 8 7 6 5 4 3 2 1   2   4 5 6 7 8/8

Printed in the U.S.A.

READ THIS FIRST

Are you ready for some really fantastic adventures with puzzles to solve, and wacky jokes too?

Start reading on **page 1** and keep going until you have to make a choice. Then decide which way you want to go, and turn to that page.

Keep going until you reach **THE END.** Then go back and take a new path. You can make the story end *lots* of different ways.

It is all up to you!

"Oh, no! Not another one!" says your dad, the chief of police in Flamingoville. He has just gotten a phone call from the mayor and he looks worried. "I know that makes the 427th plaster flamingo stolen this year. Believe me, Mayor Throckbottom, we're doing everything we can —"

Your dad comes to the breakfast table. "The mayor hung up on me," he says.

"Don't worry, Dad," you say. "It's not our fault some kook is stealing the plaster flamingos from everybody's front lawn."

"If you ask me, dear, I think the town looks nicer without them," your mother adds.

"Tell that to Mayor Throckbottom," your dad answers with a sigh. "Now that *his* flamingo has been stolen, I've got one week to solve this case or Flamingoville will have a new chief of police."

Turn to **page 2.**

Your dad gulps down his coffee. "I'd better get down to the office and see if there are any new leads."

He leaves, and a few minutes later your mom does too. She's going grocery shopping. Just you and your parakeet, Tweedles, are left at the table.

You decide to have another bowl of cereal before school, but when you pick up the box of Wonder Pops, it's almost empty. Rats! You forgot to tell Mom to buy more.

Go on to the next page.

All you get when you empty out the box are some crumbs and a cardboard triangle with funny designs on it. What is it? Some kind of prize?

You notice there's a poem on the back.

Just give a little spin
For the magic to begin.
Wherever you land
There's a power at hand.
Then spin again
For the magic to end.

Wow! A magic top! Is this for real? You've never won anything before in your entire life. Of course, this is probably some kind of joke, but you decide to try the top anyway.

Turn to the back cover of this book. Follow the directions to make your magic top. Then go back to this page and give your top a spin.

If you land on ⬱ *, turn to* **page 4.**

If you land on ⬦ *, turn to* **page 22.**

If you land on ☺ *; turn to* **page 59.**

4   You landed on ✐.

Believe it or not, you're flying.

You zoom through the living room and nearly crash into a mirror. That's when you see you have pretty blue wings and green tail feathers. Guess what! You look just like Tweedles, your parakeet!

"Holy Moley! The top works! It really is magic!" you cry. But the words come out "Tweedly tweet tweet!"

You decide to try your wings outside, so you fly out the window.

This is fun! You have a bird's-eye view of all Flamingoville. Down below you spot your dad in his police car. Hey! With this magic top, maybe you can help him solve the case of the disappearing flamingos!

When you fly by the town hall clock, you see that it's a quarter to nine. You have to get to school. You'd better get back home fast.

But can you find your way home? Things look so different from up here.

Go on to the next page.

If you come out here, turn to **page 6.**

If you come out here, turn to **page 8.**

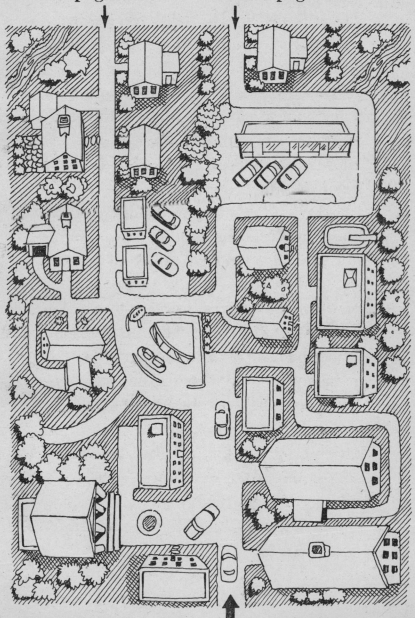

6   Oops! This isn't your house.

"Pretty birdy! Pretty birdy!" a little old lady cries. "How did you get in?"

"I'm not a bird! I'm a kid!" you say. "And I've got to be going now."

That top! You remember the poem. If you don't get back and spin the top again, the power won't end. You'll be stuck in these feathers forever! "Help," you shout. "Let me out of here!"

"How sweetly the pretty birdy sings," the lady says, shutting the window.

She decides to keep you for a pet. She calls you Peepsy and buys the fanciest birdcage in town.

What a rotten turn of events! You can't stand the taste of birdseed, and the other parakeet the lady gets to keep you company pecks at you all day long.

All you can do is hope the door to the cage and a window will be open at the same time. Then maybe you can escape and get back to that crazy magic top. In the meantime, this life is for the birds!

THE END

8   You're back in your own house.

You find the top, spin it again, and when it stops you're back to normal. Wow! You still can't get over it. That magic top really works.

You toss the top into your knapsack along with your books and homework, grab your lunchbox, and head for school.

On the way, every house you pass has a big hole out in front where its flamingo used to be. It's really too bad. The only thing Flamingoville was ever famous for was the plaster flamingo in every yard, and now there's not even one in sight.

Go on to the next page.

Hey! Wait a minute! You *do* see one flamingo. It's standing on the lawn of old Orville Pettigrew's house. How come his hasn't been stolen? Maybe the robber is scared of Mr. Pettigrew. He is a pretty creepy guy. For years he has kept to himself. The shutters of his house are always closed, and a big sign out front says GO AWAY! THIS MEANS YOU!

That's funny. You notice that the door at the side of his house is open. You wonder what's going on inside.

If you decide to investigate,
turn to **page 10.**

If you're scared of Mr. Pettigrew as
well as of teachers who make you
stay after school for being late,
keep walking and turn to **page 30.**

10   You sneak up to the open door and peek inside. Nothing. Not a sign of anyone anywhere.

You take a step inside the house and hear loud noises coming from the basement. It sounds like someone is smashing china plates . . . or maybe plaster flamingos.

You think you may be onto something. You take the top out of your knapsack. Now seems a good time for some magic powers. You give the top a spin.

If you land on ✐, turn to **page 52.**

If you land on ⟨O⟩, turn to **page 13.**

If you land on ☺ , turn to **page 25.**

"Well, I have some good news and bad news," he tells you. "The good news is that your dad's not so dumb after all. He found all the flamingos at the studio of that wacky artist Stretch Kanvass. The one who moved into town last month. It turns out he hates pink and wanted to paint all the flamingos purple. But your dad got there in time."

"That's great," you say. "What could be the bad news?"

"The bad news," Nelson says with glee, "is that I'm not giving you back your clothes!"

THE END

The top lands on ⟨○⟩.

Suddenly the gloomy old house gets much brighter. That's because you can see sunlight streaming in through the walls. It's as if they're made of glass, not concrete!

You tiptoe across the floor till you are standing over the spot where the noise is coming from. Then you look down.

With your incredible X-ray vision you can see right into the basement.

Plaster flamingos are everywhere. Old Mr. Pettigrew is busy knocking their heads off, one by one. Each time he looks into the broken hollow body, he stamps his foot.

He's looking for something, but it seems he hasn't found it yet.

Just then he puts down his hammer and starts up the stairs. He looks tired and very dusty.

Oh, brother. You'd better hide fast.

Turn to **page 14.**

14   You duck behind a beat-up sofa.

When Mr. Pettigrew walks by, you're sure he can see you. Then you remember. He's not the one with X-ray vision. *You* are.

"Dad blast it. I still haven't found the right one," he shouts.

He goes upstairs. You look up and, through the ceiling, you see him climbing into a big four-poster bed. No wonder he's tired, stealing all those flamingos!

Quickly and quietly you sneak downstairs to the basement. There must be hundreds of flamingos here, and they all seem to be staring right at you. You shudder. They almost look alive.

Go on to the next page.

You pick up an old newspaper clipping that's lying on the floor. It says:

**THIEF CAUGHT IN
FLAMINGO FACTORY**

Jake (Lightfingers) La Rue was caught by the police today in the Flyright Flamingo Factory after stealing the only one million dollar bill ever printed from the Eversafe Bank of America. When La Rue was captured, there was no sign of the money. Police are still searching the area. A $50,000 reward is being offered.

Suddenly it all clicks. The bill must be inside a flamingo. Mr. Pettigrew has been trying to find the stolen money. Pretty crafty. But maybe you can beat him to it.

Turn to **page 24.**

16   One of these flamingos is different
from the others. That's the one with the
money inside.

Can you find it?

If so, turn to **page 20.**

YIPES! You're invisible. That's what the funny little dotted figure meant. The top really is magic!

The top! It's in the trash compactor. Now that poem flashes back to you — "spin again for the power to end." But there's no top anymore. Oh, no!

"I'm leaving," your mom warns, "if I don't see you down here in one second!"

If she doesn't see you . . . HA!

"You go without me, Mom," you shout down. Somehow you're not ready to show her the new you. "And while you're at it, how about buying every box of Wonder Pops in the store."

Maybe somewhere, in another box of cereal, you'll find another magic top . . . maybe.

THE END

Good for you! You spotted the right flamingo. It's the one with the dollar sign in its left eye.

You grab the flamingo and hide in a dark corner behind the furnace. The old man comes back down to the basement and starts bashing up more flamingos.

"Rats!" he shouts. "That money is inside one of you. And I'm going to find it or my real name isn't Jake Lightfingers La Rue."

So Mr. Pettigrew is Jake La Rue, the bank robber! Now it all makes sense. He's trying to find the stolen money he hid so long ago.

Luckily the phone rings. Jake La Rue drops his hammer and stomps upstairs. Now's your chance. You've got to get out of here with the flamingo — and fast.

But if you go back up to the living room, La Rue will spot you. Your X-ray vision helps you once again. It shows you there is another way out.

Turn to **page 58.**

When Nelson reaches the mayor's fancy house, he goes around back to an old shed. It has a sign on it saying:

```
Nelson's Clubhouse
Members Only
```

What a joke! Nobody would be in any club Nelson started.

He goes inside.

You train your eyes on the door. Guess what you see in the "clubhouse"!

To find out, turn to **page 34.**

22   You landed on ⬭. What power will it give you?

"Oh, no!" you think, looking in your lunchbox. "Not another liverwurst sandwich." That makes the fourth one this week.

Hey! What's going on? Your lunchbox is shut. Yet you can see right inside it!

You have X-ray vision. What do you know! That top really is magic. Maybe it can help your dad with his case.

You walk outside. Next door in the Fullers' kitchen, you can see Mr. Fuller hiding behind his newspaper, making faces at Mrs. Fuller.

Across the street, inside old Mrs. Maypole's house, you see Tabby, her cat, trying to tip over the goldfish bowl. Should you warn her? No, you can't. There's no way to explain how you know what is happening. Besides, you see that her hall clock says it's ten to nine. Time for school. Helping your father with his case will have to wait.

Turn to **page 8.**

24   You pick up the hammer. Oh, no! That will wake him up.

Then you remember. Of course. You can just use your X-ray eyes.

You look in one flamingo after another — no million dollar bill. Finally there are only six left. Uh-oh! You can hear Mr. Pettigrew moving around. He must be up, and that means he will be *down* any second. You've got to work fast.

Turn to **page 16.**

You land on ☺ .

Great flying flamingos! You're invisible. You pinch your arm. Ouch! You feel it, but all you can see is your Mickey Mouse watch.

Hmmmmm. Being invisible will help you find out what old Mr. Pettigrew is up to, you think.

Quickly you take off your knapsack and clothes, and hide them behind the curtains.

You sneak over to the basement stairs. Then you remember that you don't have to sneak around. No one can see you.

Down in the basement old Mr. Pettigrew is busy smashing up plaster flamingos into millions of tiny pieces.

So he *is* the culprit. But why is he doing this?

Turn to **page 26.**

"Hooray!" shouts Mr. Pettigrew. "One more flamingo down. Only 323 more to go. Then there will be no ugly flamingos left in Flamingoville, and this town can finally get a sensible name. Someday they'll thank Orville Grimsly Pettigrew," he mutters. "Maybe they'll even rename the town for me!"

Crash! He breaks another flamingo with his hammer. Uh-oh! It's so dusty down here from all the bits of plaster. You feel a sneeze coming on.

"ACHOO!"

"Who's there?" Mr. Pettigrew yelps in fright. He looks white as a ghost. Hmm. That gives you an idea.

Turn to **page 28.**

Soon your dad arrives and takes Mr. Pettigrew down to headquarters. You find your knapsack where you had hidden it behind the curtains, take out the top, and give it a spin.

Right away you're not invisible anymore. Now you're dressed in your birthday suit! You get dressed and hurry off to school, where you have to pretend it's just another average day.

That night your dad is all smiles. The case has been solved. And you've still got your magic top. Ready for the next time you need it!

THE END

"Leave those flamingos alone!" you call out in a spooky voice.

"Come out, whoever you are." Mr. Pettigrew is shaking like a leaf. "I'm going to get you," he warns. He raises his hammer again, but you grab it out of his hand and drop it on his foot.

"Ouch," he cries.

Then you grab a flamingo and run around the basement. It looks as if the flamingo is flying!

"A ghost! A ghost!" screams Mr. Pettigrew. "Stop. I'll do anything you want."

"March upstairs and call the chief of police right now," you order in your spooky voice. "Tell him you are sorry and will replace every flamingo you've broken and return all the other ones."

The old man does as he's told.

Turn to **page 27.**

30   You decide you'd better go straight to school.

Later, during recess, the mayor's son, Nelson Throckbottom, Jr., starts picking on you. He's always been the meanest kid in your class.

"My dad says your father's all washed up in Flamingoville if he doesn't solve the case fast. And I don't think he can." Nelson starts laughing so hard he gets the hiccups.

"What do you know anyway, Nelson?" you say.

"More than you think," Nelson says mysteriously. Then he walks away.

Just what did he mean by that? you keep asking yourself.

When school is over, you notice Nelson hurrying off. He looks as if he's scared that someone may be following him.

You decide to see what Nelson is up to.

Go on to the next page.

You follow Nelson for a couple of blocks. All of a sudden he turns around quickly. Oops! Has he spotted you?

It looks like this might be a good time to use your magic top. You take it out of your knapsack and give it a spin.

If you land on ✒, turn to **page 44.**

If you land on ◁▷, turn to **page 32.**

If you land on ☺, turn to **page 48.**

32 You landed on ⟨O⟩.

You have X-ray vision.

Now you can see that inside Nelson's briefcase is a big hammer. What does he need that for?

At Oscar's Flaming O Burger Pit, Nelson goes inside. You wait near the door, hidden behind some bushes. Boy, are you hungry! And you even have a coupon for a free flameburger. You pull it out of your pocket and gaze at it.

FOR A BURGER THAT TASTES
LIKE
A MILLION DOLLARS
LOOK IN
THE FLAMING O

OSCAR'S BURGER PIT / GOOD FOR 1 FLAME BURGER

Should you go in now and use it? Or will Nelson get suspicious if he sees you?

If you want to go inside and get your free flameburger, turn to **page 38.**

If you decide to stay where you are and wait for Nelson to leave, turn to **page 45.**

"Hold it right there, kid!" you hear a voice behind you say. "Just where do you think you're going with that flamingo?"

It's a policeman. One you don't know.

"B-b-but, Officer," you stammer.

"No buts about it," the officer says. "You're coming downtown for questioning."

"Fine with me," you say happily.

Turn to **page 56.**

34   Flamingos everywhere!

Nelson begins smashing one up with his hammer.

So *he* is the thief! But why is he doing this?

Just then Nelson takes a torn piece of paper out of his pocket and looks it over carefully. It seems to be very important. There's some writing on it, but even with your X-ray eyes it's hard to read what it says.

You squint harder.

Now you can make out what's on the paper.

FOR

A MILLION DOLLARS
LOOK IN
THE FLAMING O

Hmmm. There's something awfully familiar about those words. You're sure you've seen them before. But where?

Think about it for a while.
Then go on to the next page.

You've figured it out.

"Hold it, Nelson!" you shout, storming into the barn. "Don't touch another flamingo."

"Get out of here, pipsqueak," Nelson cries. "I'm going to find a million dollars in one of these dumb birds."

"Oh, no, you're not," you say. "Those flamingos are as empty as your head."

"Yeah? Take a look at this," he says, shoving the torn paper in your face.

"Yeah? Well, take a look at *this!*" you shout back.

You whip out your flameburger coupon and stick it under Nelson's nose.

"Now do you get it?" you ask Nelson. But it's obvious he's still in the dark.

"Look, Nelson," you tell him. "Just follow the directions. Then you'll see."

Turn to **page 36.**

Use a pen or pencil to black out all the words to the right of this dotted line.

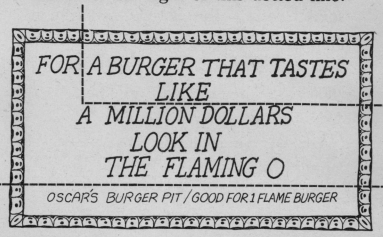

FOR A BURGER THAT TASTES LIKE
A MILLION DOLLARS
LOOK IN
THE FLAMING O

OSCAR'S BURGER PIT / GOOD FOR 1 FLAME BURGER

Black out everything below this dotted line.

What do you see now?

Go on to the next page.

"Oh, no!" Nelson cries.

"Oh, yes! You don't have a clue for some treasure. You just have a torn coupon from Oscar's Flaming O. . . . And, boy, is your dad going to be mad when *my* dad tells him who the flamingo thief was!"

Case closed.

THE END

38   You get your flameburger and sit at one of the back tables at Oscar's. Nelson doesn't seem to have spotted you. Good!

Over at the next table, there's the strangest looking guy. He's wearing a bright pink silk jacket, and his hair has a bright pink streak in the front. Leaning against the empty chair facing him is a huge case for a bass violin.

Wow! It's Pinky, the guitar player from Punk Flamingo, your favorite group. You have all their records.

What is Pinky doing here in Flamingoville?

And what is he doing with that big bass violin case when he plays guitar?

If you want to find out more about Pinky, turn to **page 40.**

If you still think Nelson is the key to the missing flamingos, turn to **page 45.**

40   You stare at Pinky's bass violin case.

With your sharp X-ray vision you are beginning to make out what is inside the case . . . and it's not a bass violin!

Start at 1. Then connect all the dots on the next page.

Do you see it clearly now? Why it's a —

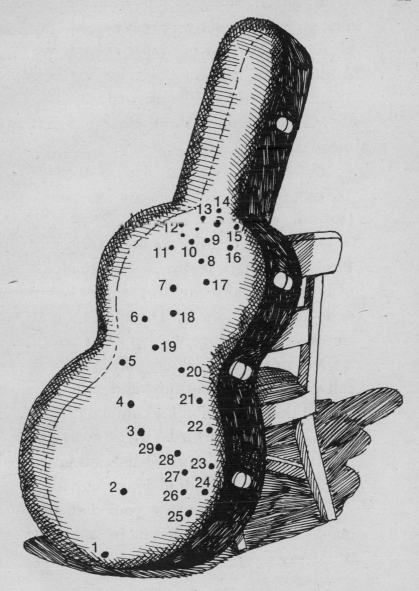

Turn to **page 60.**

"Don't get so upset, it's just a joke," Pinky says. "We haven't really stolen the flamingos. We just borrowed them so we could photograph the cover for our new album — 'Live at Flamingoville.' "

"Wait a minute. Punk Flamingo has never played here," you say.

"But we're going to. This Saturday. We're giving a free concert for every-body in town."

"No fooling!" you shout. "Terrific." Punk Flamingo really are a bunch of okay guys. Then you remember your dad. "Er, look, fellas. The mayor's real sore at my father for not solving this case."

"No problem," Pinky says. "We'll call your father right now and confess."

Your dad makes Punk Flamingo return all the "borrowed birds" right away.

Pinky keeps his word. The band gives a great concert for all of Flamingoville.

Everybody is happy — your dad, the mayor, and most of all you. In fact, you could say everything is just tops.

THE END

44   You landed on ✏.

Just before the top stopped, a fly buzzed by. And guess what, that's just what you are now too! You've got two antennae, six furry legs, and tiny wings.

You buzz over Nelson the rest of the way home and fly in through an open window.

Oops! You're in the mayor's den, and Mayor Throckbottom himself is talking on the phone.

"My kid just walked in the house. We better make this fast," Mayor Throckbottom says to the person on the other end of the line. "Yes, I know. This is the best publicity stunt I've ever thought of. Stealing all the flamingos is sure to put Flamingoville on the map. Now, if only that thick-headed police chief would discover them down by the lake. I even had my secretary call him today with an anonymous tip. By tonight we should be a front-page story in newspapers everywhere. And then — hello, tourists!"

Turn to **page 47.**

At last, after wolfing down three flame-burgers and four supershakes, Nelson leaves Oscar's. You are right behind him.

Turn to **page 21.**

So that's it. The mayor cooked up this whole thing just to make Flamingoville famous.

Right away you decide to fly back to where you left the top, so you can turn back into yourself and let your dad know what's going on. To think how worried he's been! It really makes you mad. You start buzzing like crazy.

Uh oh! That was *not* a good move.

The mayor has suddenly grabbed a newspaper. "Wait a minute," he says into the phone. "There's a pesty fly around here. I'm going to swat it."

He means you!

You head for the window. The mayor is right behind! You'd better make a fast getaway or this could be

THE END

48   You land on ☺ .

Before you can say "fifty flying flamingos," you're invisible. And here you
are at Nelson's house. Quickly you get
out of your clothes and knapsack and stuff
them in the Throckbottoms' mailbox.
You'll have to remember to get them
later.

You walk right beside Nelson all the
way up to his front door.

When he stops to get his key, you reach
over and tickle him in the ribs.

"Who did that?" he yells.

You tickle him again and then tweak
his nose. That was for the time Nelson
poured glue in your gym shoes. Nelson
keeps waving his arms, looking for the
culprit. But of course he can't see any-
body!

"Must be some crazy mosquitos
around," Nelson mutters, opening the
door and slamming it right in your face.

Too bad. You should have seen that
one coming.

Go on to the next page.

You walk around the house looking for   **49**
an open window to climb through. Rats!
They're all locked. At one window you
can see the mayor in his den. He's talking
on the phone. All of a sudden Nelson
comes into the room.

You press your invisible ear close to
the glass and try hard to hear what they're
saying.

Toss a coin.
If it comes up heads,
turn to **page 50**.

If it comes up tails,
turn to **page 53**.

You can only hear bits of what the mayor is telling Nelson.

"Just got a call . . . all over . . . soon the whole town will know . . . front page in tonight's paper."

What does this mean? It sure sounds like the flamingo mystery is solved. Is your dad a hero?

Nelson looks as surprised at the news as you are. He must have been bluffing at school. He didn't know any more about the mystery than you did.

"Sure, Dad," you can hear Nelson saying. "I'll check right now to see if the paper's here."

Nelson leaves his father's den. It takes you a second or two to realize he's heading for the mailbox.

Go on to the next page.

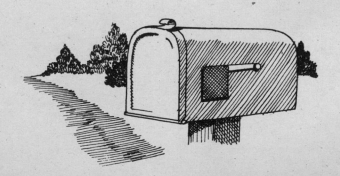

Oh, no! That's where you left your clothes and knapsack.

You race around to the front of the house. But Nelson has beaten you to it.

"What's this?" Nelson says to himself.

With horror you watch him take the top from your knapsack and give it a spin.

Guess who's not invisible anymore!

Has Nelson spotted you? You jump behind one of Mrs. Throckbottom's prize rosebushes.

"OUCH!" you yelp. Those thorns don't tickle.

Nelson spins around.

"What on earth are you doing here? Like *that!*" he shouts.

"Nelson, I can explain. . . . But first tell me about the flamingos," you say. "I've got to know."

There's a wicked gleam in Nelson's eye.

Turn to **page 11.**

Poof! You've turned into a bird! An eagle! Just like the stuffed one in the corner. Suddenly you have a tremendous urge to fly out the window and go soaring through the treetops. But that's not what you're here for. You're supposed to see what Mr. Pettigrew is up to.

You hop over to the top and, with great difficulty, use your beak to spin the top again. You turn back into a kid and spin once more. Maybe this time you'll land on another magic power.

If you land on ✒️ again,
stay on this page.

If you land on 👁️ , go to **page 13.**

If you land on ☺ , go to **page 25.**

You hear snatches of conversation.

"Any news about the flamingos?" Nelson asks his father. You can tell from his voice he doesn't know a thing. He must have been teasing you at school. Pretending he knew a lot. That Nelson!

Mayor Throckbottom shakes his head no and you realize that following Nelson has been a big waste of time.

You find your clothes and knapsack. As soon as you spin the top you're no longer invisible.

Gee, it's later than you thought. You'd better get home fast. You've got a lot of homework to do. You decide to take a shortcut through Paradise Park.

All of a sudden you look down and see a single set of tracks . . . flamingo tracks!

You follow them. A while later they're joined by another set of tracks . . . and then another . . . and another. Pretty soon there are so many tracks, you can't tell them apart. Your heart is pounding. What's going on here?

To find out, turn to **page 54.**

You come over the top of a hill, and there, standing in the twilight by Paradise Pond, are the missing flamingos . . . all 427 of them. The only thing is that they're not made of plaster. They are absolutely real!

One turns its head and looks at you. It has a black circle around its right eye. Just like the one you painted, as a joke, on the flamingo that used to stand in your yard.

Somehow you know what's going to happen next.

"Good-bye!" you call out. There is a loud whoosh of wings as the flamingos take off into the sunset. A few seconds later, they're gone.

You've found out what happened to all the flamingos. Too bad no one will ever believe it!

THE END

56   Ten minutes later you're in your father's office.

"Dad! Dad!" you shout. "I've solved the case. Orville Pettigrew stole all the flamingos. Only he's really not Orville Pettigrew. He's the bank robber, Jake La Rue. He hid a million dollar bill inside this flamingo. Where's a hammer?"

You can tell your father doesn't quite believe you, but he gets a hammer anyway. Crash! The flamingo is in a million pieces. The money is staring right at you.

"The money from the Eversafe Bank holdup!" your dad exclaims. He sends an officer to go pick up La Rue. Then your dad rubs his chin. "It's not that I'm playing favorites, but as far as I can see, there's just one person who deserves that $50,000 reward — YOU!"

Wow! Everything sure worked out great. Your dad's job is safe and you're a local hero, especially after you spend some of your reward money replacing all the flamingos that got smashed.

Go on to the next page.

"Just tell me," your dad asks later. "How did you know which flamingo had the money inside?"

"I owe it all to Wonder Pops," you say with a mysterious smile. "It really is the breakfast of heros!"

THE END

58   Some steps lead from the basement out into the backyard.

Soon you're outside and running down the block as fast as you can. Boy! This flamingo weighs a ton.

Turn to **page 33.**

You landed on ☺ . What amazing power will you get? With your magic top, maybe you can help your dad solve the case of the disappearing flamingos. You wait for a minute. Nothing happens. You wait a minute more. Still nothing. Some magic! You should have known not to expect much from a box of Wonder Pops.

Feeling annoyed, you toss the top and the empty cereal box into the trash compactor. Then you go upstairs to get ready for school.

You hear somebody downstairs.

"It's just me," your mom says. "I forgot my coupons for the supermarket." *WHHHRRRR* goes the sound of the trash compactor. "Hurry and I'll drive you to school."

"Be right down," you yell. Passing the mirror in the upstairs hall, you see yourself. . . . Or to be more exact, you *don't* see yourself. Your baseball cap is there. So are your jeans, your knapsack, and your T-shirt. The only thing that's missing is YOU!

Turn to **page 19.**

60   A pink plaster flamingo!

You can hardly believe your X-ray eyes!

When Pinky leaves Oscar's you do too. It's easy to trail him. He can't go too fast, not with that heavy bass violin case.

A few blocks from Oscar's, in an old part of Flamingoville, Pinky suddenly ducks into a big abandoned warehouse. The windows are all boarded up, but that doesn't stop *you* from seeing inside.

Just as you thought!

There's Pinky and the rest of the band surrounded by all the missing flamingos!

You burst inside the warehouse.

"Hold it," a man with a big camera is telling the band. "This shot looks perfect."

"No! You hold it, you dirty thieves," you shout. "Just what is going on here? Why did you take our flamingos?"

Turn to **page 42.**